NIC

of the Woods

NIC
of the Woods

by LYND WARD

HOUGHTON MIFFLIN COMPANY

Wa
Feb '68

NIC

of the Woods

Chapter 1

DAVID WOODS' dog was not the biggest dog on the block and he wasn't the smallest, either. But Davey was sure he was the smartest.

His mother was a show-ring cocker spaniel whose name was Black Diamond. Nobody called her that, of course. She was known as Dime. And because the puppy was only half as big when they took him home, naturally his name was Nickel. So nobody ever called him anything but Nic.

Davey didn't want to have Nic's tail cut short, as show-ring cockers' tails are supposed to be. So Nic's tail grew long and plumy. And then his legs grew long too, much longer than cockers' are supposed to be.

So in addition to being smart, Nic was soon the fastest runner on the block. He allowed no other animal on the Woods' place. He was very good at chasing other dogs out of the yard, no matter how big they were. He was very good with squirrels too and even an occasional cat.

Every summer the Woods went up to Canada where they had a cabin on the shore of Lonely Lake. Nic, of course, had never been on a train before. He wasn't very happy when someone fastened a big baggage tag to his collar and tied him in a corner of the baggage car, where he jolted along with the trunks and crates.

It was hard to tell who was happier, Nic or Davey, when the train finally stopped and they were together again.

Mr. Watson was waiting for them with his team and wagon, as he was every year. After they had loaded up, they drove slowly over the long hill and down the other side. The barnyards they passed had more strange animals in them than Nic had ever seen before.

Then it was up another hill and the farms were left far behind. The road pushed its way through thick tangles of trees. They grew so close to the road that even Davey could reach up and pick off a branch from a low-hanging maple. Nic sniffed a new smell in the air and Davey waited for his father to say, as he did every year when they got that far, "Well, sir, now the Woods are really in the woods."

It was a good fifteen miles from the station to the lake and then they had to put everything in the boat and row two miles up the lake. They couldn't even see their boathouse until they were through the narrows. Nic had never been in a boat before, so Davey had to keep telling him how to behave.

"No running from side to side. No jumping up and down. Just sit quietly till we get to the dock, and then don't get out until you are told to."

The first job was to get the cabin open and all the suitcases and
boxes of supplies carried up from the dock. Then Davey put on
his camp clothes and tucked his trouser legs into the tops of his
shoepacs so they wouldn't catch in the underbrush. He unbuckled
Nic's collar.

"Well, sir," said Davey, "being in the woods is different from down home. No collar and no leash."

Mrs. Woods said, "Now that you are both ready for the woods, why not go over and tell Professor Cook we're here?"

Professor Cook had the only other cabin on the lake. His camp was a good half mile away, way down in a deep bay. You couldn't even see it until you got well around the point.

When they got around the point there was Professor Cook tied up to his favorite snag, fishing.

He had on his fisherman's hat and he waved and called to Davey that he was delighted to see him and to meet Nic. He had a message for Mrs. Woods.

"Tell your mother I have a fish for your supper — and it's big enough for all four of you."

"Thank you very much," said Davey. "We're going to say hello to Mr. McWaters."

Davey explained to Nic that Tom McWaters was Professor Cook's cook. He worked in lumber camps every winter and then worked for Professor Cook every summer, because Professor Cook had no family. But it wasn't easy to make pies by the dozen and cookies by the hundreds for fifty hungry loggers all winter and then suddenly cut down to just one fisherman, even as big a one as Professor Cook. So Mr. McWaters always ended up with far too many things to eat. He was pleased when Davey came over to help with the cookie problem.

"Well, sir," said Davey, "from now on there will be two of us to help with the cookie problem."

When they were almost home they stopped off at the swimming dock. Davey had some things to say.

"For someone who has never been in the woods before you are doing pretty well. But you have a lot to learn. The reason you have to stay close to heel when we go along a trail, and not run ahead or dash off to the side is because you can get lost in these woods. You've got to remember what my father says I have got to remember. If you do get lost don't get worried and upset. Someone will be looking for you. So don't wear yourself out running in circles. And remember you can always find some berries or something like that to keep your strength up.

"But we'll be doing other things besides going through the woods. We will be going fishing, and we have to get minnows and frogs; and tomorrow we'll put the ladder on the swimming dock and put up the springboard and then go swimming."

Chapter 2

THE NEXT DAY when they went in swimming Davey dove head-first off the springboard. His mother's eyes opened wide in astonishment.

"I didn't know you could do that!" she cried.

His father gave a big yell. "Wow! This is a surprise. Last year you went in feet first and you had to hold your nose."

Nic was surprised too. When he saw Davey disappear under-water he got very upset. He whined and barked and kept it up until Davey was safely back on the dock. Davey's mother put her hands over her ears.

"David, my boy," said his father, "that dog of yours has a lot to learn — and he might start with not being so noisy."

They went hunting for frogs. But Nic couldn't seem to get the idea that you had to sneak up on them slowly and quietly or they were gone before you even saw where.

For minnows they had to go out on the end of the dock. "Here's the idea," said Davey, "you let the net settle slowly into the water. Then you drop little bread balls onto the center of the net. When enough minnows are busy with the bread you pull it up with a 'whoosh' and get the net onto the dock. Then you move fast to dump the minnows into the bucket before they flop back in the lake."

Davey discovered that it didn't help much to have a dog bouncing around trying to get a mouthful of minnows on his own.

When they went fishing there were problems, too. The day Davey was reeling in a bigger bass than he had ever hooked before, Nic went right out of the boat into the lake.

"For the love of Pete," cried Davey, "that's no help!"

But his father said he didn't think Nic was trying to help. He just couldn't wait to get a mouthful of bass.

Then one morning when Davey was busy carrying in wood for the kitchen stove there was a burst of frantic barking from the edge of the woods. When Davey got there he found that it was only a squirrel. Nic was in a fury because the squirrel didn't run away silently and hide the way squirrels did back home. This fellow stayed just out of reach no matter how high Nic jumped. And what was worse, he kept talking back in a loud excited chatter such as Nic had never heard before.

The next animal Nic met in the woods didn't say a word. This one looked very much like one of the occasional cats Nic had chased out of the yard at home. Nic stopped and the stranger stopped. Then Nic's ears went back, a low rumbling growl started deep down in his throat, and burst into a loud bark. The stranger stamped his little front feet up and down. As the dog sprang forward the stranger swung around back to, lifted his tail, and did something that no cat of Nic's acquaintance had ever done.

First they tried soap and water, but the fur was more skunky wet than dry. Professor Cook said when he was a boy they used to cover a skunked dog with dirt to get the smell off. So they buried Nic in dirt with only his head sticking out. For three hours Davey kept patting him and talking to him to keep him quiet. But when he finally shook free of the dirt the smell wasn't much better.

Mr. McWaters said try washing him with kerosene. Davey's father said, "Someone once told me you can get it off with tomatoes." So they rubbed two cans of stewed tomatoes into the worst places and it still wasn't much better.

Then Davey's mother said, "Try lilac water." But even when her whole big bottle was emptied over him Nic still smelled mainly of skunk. So Davey went back to soap and water and scrubbed him over and over five days in a row. And with each bath, Davey said, "Nic, you have a lot to learn. But you will."

Davey had to hold him tight so he wouldn't struggle while Mr. Woods took a pair of pliers and pulled the quills out one at a time.

Mrs. Woods said she couldn't bear to watch. When the quills were all out Mr. Woods said, "Davey, my boy, Nic still has a lot to learn about being a real woods dog. You'd better have a heart-to-heart talk with him."

The best place for a heart-to-heart talk was down the trail a way where there was a big rock covered with ferns and moss. It was just about big enough for a boy and a dog.

"Well, sir," said Davey, "it seems you still have things to learn. This isn't like at home. You don't have to chase everything out of the yard. These animals all live here, and if we leave them alone they leave us alone. So you've just got to learn how to behave in the woods and in boats. We're going to spend a whole week with Professor Cook out on Lake Algoma. We will be fishing for big lake trout and there will be new things to see and picnics on islands. How much fun will it be if you keep getting into trouble this way?"

Chapter 3

But the day before they were to leave for the trip on the big lake Davey's father said he and Davey had to have a heart-to-heart talk.

"Professor Cook thinks a dog wouldn't be very happy cooped up on a boat for a whole week. He says Nic can stay with Tom McWaters. And I guess if you think about it that way you can see it would be better."

Davey didn't really think it would be better that way. But the morning they were to leave he put Nic's collar and leash on and took him over to the Cook Camp. He gave Mr. McWaters a big box of dog biscuit and explained about feeding twice a day and the bowl of water a dog always liked even if the lake was a good place to drink, too.

Professor Cook kept his motorboat on Big Moose River. Davey
and his father and mother packed the things they needed for the
trip in their knapsacks and started up the trail to Long Lake. Long
Lake was over the ridge behind the cabin and the Woods had a
boathouse over there, too. They rowed to the far end of that
lake where there was an old lumber road. For five miles they had
to clamber over old bridges and scramble over fallen trees, but

the road finally brought them to an abandoned farm with over-
grown fields that ran down to Big Moose River. There, sitting
on a big stump, was Professor Cook, waiting for them.

His motorboat was tied to a little dock someone had built out into the river. Professor Cook had on his sailor's sweater and his captain's cap. His boat was a cruiser named *School's Out*. It was thirty-six feet long and had bunks up forward for sleeping, a galley behind the engine, and a covered cockpit with cushioned seats all around.

Professor Cook was a good navigator. It took careful work to steer safely down Big Moose River. Davey's job was to keep an eye on the dinghy and see that it was towing all right and didn't get its line fouled in the propeller as they made a sharp turn or slowed down suddenly. But when they got out in the main channel there were new things to see. He kept one eye on the dinghy and with the other took in the sights — islands, summer cottages and boathouses, fishermen on the rocky points, and a few boats with girls and boys.

When they got out on Lake Algoma there were more gulls and buoys and every once in a while an ore boat going north to Lake Superior for another load of ore.

Toward sunset they found an island and Professor Cook baked a big trout over a campfire. At times like this Davey couldn't help feeling it wasn't better this way at all. He kept wondering what Nic was doing and how he was getting on.

Chapter 4

WHEN Nic saw Davey go off down the trail he whimpered a little, then lay down quietly near the stove. Mr. McWaters fastened the leash to a nail behind the woodbox, took a dog biscuit out of the box and gave it to him. Nic turned his head away.

Then Mr. McWaters got a bowl of water and put it down near him. Nic didn't touch it.

Next Mr. McWaters took some dog biscuits and broke them up into pieces and mixed them with a can of beef stew and gravy. Nic didn't even sniff at it. In desperation Mr. McWaters got out two of his biggest cookies and held them close to the dog's nose. Nic didn't move. Mr. McWaters was at his wits' end. He thought: Maybe it's because he's tied up?

So he reached down and unsnapped the leash. He had no sooner straightened up when Nic was on his feet like a flash, out of the open kitchen door and hightailing it down the trail for home.

When Nic got back to the Woods' cabin he ran first to one door, then to another. They were closed tightly. He ran down to the boathouse. There was no one there. He ran up to the cabin again, and sat for a while at the back door waiting.

Then he started sniffing around and soon was following the trail up the hill, then down the other side to the boathouse on Long Lake. When the faint smells he was following seemed to end on the dock he sat down and waited. Toward sunset he gave up and went back over the trail to the cabin.

Suddenly he saw Mr. McWaters coming up from the boathouse, calling his name. Nic got one look at the leash he carried and slunk off into the woods without a sound.

Several times the next day Mr. McWaters came back looking and calling. Nic never let him get very close. The last time he came Mr. McWaters brought a bowl of food and left it by the back door.

When Mr. McWaters was gone Nic waited a while, then approached carefully and started eating. Suddenly he stopped.

From far off he heard a call.

He raced up the trail and over the hill. But when he got near the boathouse on Long Lake he saw that the sounds were coming from a pair of loons. They were splashing and diving close to shore, and every once in a while the loons gave short calls that were almost human.

Nic started walking slowly through the trees along the shore.

After a while Nic found himself way up on a big rock where he could look out across the whole of Long Lake. At the far end he saw what looked like a rowboat drawn up on the shore.

It took him quite a while to work his way around to it and find the old lumber road.

It took a while longer to follow that road across the old broken bridges and finally to the abandoned farm.

At last he reached the little dock built out into the river. He waited there a long time.

But nobody came. Finally Nic decided nobody was going to come and started back through the woods. He found that going in this direction the old lumber road wasn't quite as easy to follow. There were other roads that branched off in different directions and smaller trails that seemed to offer shortcuts. He wasn't sure which was the right way to go.

Several times he met an animal coming in the opposite direction. Then he stopped, looked at the stranger and carefully moved off the trail to walk past without bothering him.

Sometimes this took him so far off the trail that Nic had a hard time remembering which way he was heading. He seemed to be going in circles. The path grew rougher, the hills were steeper; there were more rocks, and getting over the fallen trees became harder and harder. He was very tired.

And then suddenly right in front of him stood an animal he had never seen before.

Nic's ears went back. That low rumbling growl started deep down in his throat but then for the first time it didn't burst into a loud bark.

Chapter 5

WHEN the week on the boat was over, the three Woods tramped the long five miles back to their own lake. When they got there, the first thing Davey did was to take off for Cook Camp as hard as he could go.

Mr. McWaters told him Nic wasn't there and explained what had happened. Davey went back along the trail even faster.

When Davey told them about it his mother caught her breath sharply, "You mean Nic has been out in the woods for all this time?" she cried.

Davey's father looked very serious, "Come on," he said. "We've got to find him."

They rowed carefully around the shore of the lake, close in around every point, deep into every bay. Davey kept calling, "Here Nic! Here Nic! Come on, Nic!" as loud as he could. And every so often Mr. Woods would join in, "Here Nic! Here Nic!"

But there was no answering bark. No dog came running.

The next day they did the same thing on the other lake, going farther along both shores than even Mr. Woods had ever been. There was no answer to their calling.

They went along the trails and old lumber roads as far as they could manage, calling Nic's name, first Davey, then his father, all day long. They got farther back in the forest than any of them had ever been before, into places where the trees were taller and blacker than any Davey had ever seen. In the middle of calling Davey thought he heard a faint bark.

"Listen!" he cried to his father.

They were both as still as still. They heard nothing but the soft sound of the wind in the tops of the pines. Once or twice they caught the distant voice of a raucous raven. Once there was a far-off owl hooting long before it was dark.

At night when they got back to the cabin they were pretty well exhausted.

Davey's father said, "David, my boy, we've done all the looking we can. If Nic was still around he would have heard us by now, or we would have heard him. In the woods things happen sometimes. There is not much anyone can do. You're big enough to understand that now."

Davey went out to the big rock to try to figure out some way he could stay on at the lake after his folks went back home. Then if Nic was just off somewhere and could find his way back in the middle of the winter, there would be someone in the cabin when he got there. His father saw him and suggested they go out fishing.

"I don't feel like it," said Davey.

Later his father said, "What about a last game of horseshoes?"

"I don't feel like it," said Davey.

Finally, his father came along with a couple of pails. "Davey, my boy, we have just about time to go over to the clearing and get some raspberries to take back home with us."

All Davey could say was, "I don't feel like it." But he went.

The clearing was nearly a mile away, but it was thick with raspberries. Davey usually filled his pail almost as soon as his father did. Now he was not only slow but twice he knocked his pail over and had to spend long minutes rescuing the berries from the deep grass.

Whenever he picked close to a big stump he remembered that
bears liked raspberries too. When he thought of bears and he
thought of Nic he shivered. Then he heard something moving in
the bushes behind him. Davey sprang to his feet.

It was Nic. He came limping through the tangled bushes, so
tired he could hardly get his tail up to wag it. He rubbed his head
against Davey's arm, licked Davey's hand, then ate a handful of
raspberries Davey held out to him.

It was a long mile back to the cabin. Every few minutes Davey would give a mighty yell, "Nic's found!"

His voice was so loud that Mr. McWaters heard it all the way over at Cook Camp. And Professor Cook heard it out by his favorite snag where he was trying to get his line free from the rocks. He got so excited that he pulled too hard, broke the line, and lost it all, hook, line and sinker.

Davey's mother was busy packing suitcases and making sandwiches for the lunch they would need on the train. When she heard Davey's yell she dropped the pan of eggs she was hard-boiling and came running down the trail to meet them without even stopping to pick up the mess.

A big bowl of warm milk and a good night's sleep were all that Nic needed to fix him up.

And the next day when they got to the station and were waiting for the train, Davey's father explained to the station agent what had happened. When the train came the station agent talked to the baggage man, and so by special permission Davey rode in the baggage car with Nic all the way home. And quite often Davey

patted his head and said, "I think you've learned a lot about living in the woods."

Davey never found out where Nic had been or what had happened to him in the woods. But from that time on, whenever they met anyone in a big fur coat Nic's ears would go back, and he would start that little low growl. Then he would stop and back slowly away until he was close to Davey's side. And there he would stay.